To Summer and Ethan,

and to Anne,
who brings
our mail

a division of Penguin Putnam Books for Young Readers, 345 Hudson Street, New York, NY 10014.
G. P. Putnam's Sons, Reg. U.S. Pat. & Tm. Off. Published simultaneously in Canada. Printed in Hong Kong
by South China Printing Co. (1988) Ltd. Designed by Gunta Alexander. Text set in Poppl-Laudatio Condensed.
The art was done with Caran d'Ache neocolor watercolor crayons and acrylics.
Library of Congress Cataloging-in-Publication Data   Sloat, Teri. Hark! The aardvark angels sing: A story of
Christmas mail / Teri Sloat. p.   cm.   1. Children's songs—United States—Texts. [1. Aardvarks—Songs and music.
2. Angels—Songs and music. 3. Postal service—Songs and music. 4. Christmas music. 5. Carols—Adaptations.]
I. Title. PZ8.3.S63245 Har 2001   782.42164'0268—dc21   [E] 00-041548   ISBN 0-399-23371-7
10 9 8 7 6 5 4 3 2 1   First Impression

HARK!
The Aardvark Angels Sing

A Story of Christmas Mail

TERI SLOAT

G. P. Putnam's Sons
New York

Hark! The aardvark angels sing.
Listen, Harold's trumpeting!

Calling to his angel friends,
"Time to help with mail again!"

Straight to earth the angels fly—
Christmas mail is piling high.

They help the mailmen sort the mail,
Stamped for air and ship and rail.

Hark! The aardvark angels sing,
Loading trucks with mail to bring.

Hark! The aardvark angels know
How to help when traffic's slow.

Angels push the mailman's jeep
Where mud is deep and hills are steep.

Watch the aardvark angels go,
Breaking trails through ice and snow,

Safely leading caravans,

Guiding mail through blinding sands.

Hark! The aardvark angels fly
Mail planes through the foggy sky.

Hark! The aardvark angels glide

Through the swamps where gators hide.

Aardvark angels ride the rail,
Finding cowboys on the trail.

Angels wind through jungle trees,

Gather mail from underseas,

Come in answer to the prayers
Of the mailmen climbing stairs.

Hark! The aardvark angels bless
Mail without a street address.

Hark! The aardvark angels race
Back and forth with mail from space.

Then they hear the trumpet blow,
Announcing that it's time to go—

From Okinawa to Atlanta,
One last trip with mail for Santa.

To the North Pole Harold flies;
Angels follow through the skies.

"Merry Christmas!" angels cheer—
"And to all a great new year!"

Hark!
The Aardvark Angels Sing

Charles Wesley Felix • Mendelssohn-Bartholdy

1. Hark! The aard - vark an - gels sing.___ Lis - ten, Har - old's trum - pet - ing!
2. Hark! The aard - vark an - gels know___ How to help when traf - fic's slow.
3. Hark! The aard - vark an - gels glide___ Through the swamps where ga - tors hide.
4. Hark! The aard - vark an - gels race___ Back and forth with mail from space,

Call - ing to his an - gel friends,___ "Time to help with mail a - gain!"
An - gels push the mail - man's jeep___ Where mud is deep and hills are steep.
Aard - vark an - gels ride the rail,___ Find - ing cow - boys on the trail.
'Till they hear the trum - pet blow,___ Announc - ing that it's time to go.

Straight to earth the an - gels fly—___ Christ - mas mail is pil - ing high.___
Watch the aard - vark an - gels go,___ Break - ing trails through ice and snow,___
An - gels wind through jun - gle trees,___ Gath - er mail from un - der - seas,___
From O - kin - awa to At - lanta___ One last trip with mail for Santa.___